THE M

A TWO-PART UTOPIAN NOVELLA OF THE NEAR FUTURE

WRITTEN IN

Italiaraja, UP, India
Khajuraho, MP, India
Fredericksburg, TX, the United States
Seattle, WA, the United States
Bishkek, the Kyrgyz Republic

BETWEEN

May 2001 and October 2002
Extensively revised in
October and November 2005
and
January to August 2014

BY
WARRENHALL CRAIN

I am placing **THE MESSAGE** in your hands with my thanks to my exceptionally competent and caring editor, Lindsay Hall. Lindsay and I have now worked together to publish three books—*The Message* as well as *Aashish 1926-2034* and *Readings from an India Journal*—although we live thousands of miles apart and have not seen each other since 1956.

WarrenHall Crain
10 September, 2014

Front cover photo:

EARTHRISE (NASA/Apollo 8 Astronauts)

I've chosen this photograph for the cover of this book because it captures in one word and
one image what THE MESSAGE is all about.

WarrenHall Crain, New Year 2015

Copyright © 2014 WarrenHall Crain
All rights reserved

ISBN: 1500861219
ISBN: 978-1500861216

CONTENTS

PROLOGUE
"DANCING IN THE NIGHT SKY"

PART ONE: THE MESSAGE

I. THE EVENT (The Vernal Equinox, Sunday, 20 March 2016 CE)

1. Australia—Joe and Molly (3:30 PM)   1

2. United States—Michael (12:30 AM)   15

3. India—Chaveri (10:00 AM)   27

4. Russia—Svetlana (2:30 PM)   31

5. China—Tien Wei (12:30 PM)   35

II. THE DARK YEARS (2026–2031 CE)

1. The Assassination of Carol Obwana (1 January 2026 CE)   45

2. The Marriage of Winnie and Bonnie (6 December 2029 CE)   51

3. The Peace of Jerusalem (1 July 2031 CE)   55

III. THE NEW EARTH

    1. The State of the New Earth Address
       (1 July 2032 CE)   63

IV. DANCING IN THE NEW EARTH

    1. Michael and Chaveri
       (21 March 2033 CE)   73

PART ONE EPILOGUE: ALWAYS   79

PART TWO: WHAT, THEN, DID OCCUR?

I.   WHAT, THEN, DID OCCUR?   83
II. AASHCHARIYA—WONDER   91
III. THE TEMPLE OF THE PEOPLE   99
IV. CONSENSUS   101

PART TWO EPILOGUE: ALWAYS   105

AFTERWORD

PROLOGUE

Dancing in the Night Sky

THE RAIN FALLS gently tonight and there is no wind.
Forks of lightning pierce the dark clouds.
Surely Lord Shiva is pleased with his people
And is dancing in the night sky.

THE GOVERNMENT, TOO, is pleased tonight:
Floodlights shine late on the Chandela temples.
And the single light across the lake brings
Remembrance of pleasant days in Maniram's farmhouse.

NOW AND AGAIN behind the temples the sky lights up
And is reflected in the lake's rain dappled surface.
Now and again all round the thunder rolls,
Sounding very like the arrival of our daily Indian Airlines 737.

WRAPPED IN MY warm shawl I revel in this *lila*:
Lightning flashes in the Madhya Pradesh sky,
The Khajuraho temples are still floodlit, and
In my heart the Lord of History dances.

WarrenHall Crain
8 PM, 9 FEB 1996
Khajuraho

lila—play

Part One

The Message

I.

THE EVENT

**The Vernal Equinox
Sunday, 20 March, 2016 CE**

1. Australia

Joe and Molly
(3:30 PM, Sunday, 20 March 2016 CE)

Joe and Molly were ordinary folks—plain, simple, good people. In some parts of the world they might be referred to as "the salt of the earth." Here in Wagga Wagga where they had both lived all their lives they were not widely known. Nothing famous or special about them, though six years ago many people knew them. Joe had been captain of the high school cricket team—a team which that year had won the state cup in New South Wales. Molly had been the prettiest girl in town. She had been pleased when at the victory banquet Joe had asked her to marry him. All the other girls were jealous. And Joe had thought himself the most fortunate bloke in town when she had said yes. They had been going together for years—childhood sweethearts.

Now they had two charming children and lived in a small house in an inexpensive, though surely not run-down, section of Wagga Wagga. Close to each of their families so the grandparents could see their grand-kids often. Joe was already a deacon in the Methodist church where they were members and Molly sang in the choir. Joe worked as a custodian at the High School and never missed a cricket match there. Molly was a nurse at the City Hospital. Joe had made another pot of coffee that afternoon and now held in his hand the six

The Message ◆ Part One ◆ The Event

sheets of lined paper on which they had been told **THE MESSAGE** would appear.

The letter had seemed so strange that they had not told anybody else, though they had kept their ears open wondering whether anybody else had received the letter. It had been in a simple white business envelope with an Australian stamp, postmarked in Sidney on 15 March. No return address. Just the letters CC in plain black print in the upper left corner. No further clues as to where it might have come from. Joe had nearly thrown it in the trash without opening it, thinking it was probably some junk mail or advertising. But it was addressed to them by name:

Mr. and Mrs. Joseph Lambkin
231 West Smith Street
Wagga Wagga, New South Wales

Joe had opened the envelope to find seven sheets of fine bond paper—a brief message on the first sheet, the rest blank. It had seemed to Molly, when he showed it to her, that it might be a hoax of some sort, though she wondered why if this was simply a joke the sender had used such fine paper. And it seemed to come from someone who knew them, or at least knew their names, Joe and Molly.

ON THE FIRST page of the seven were the following words:

Joe and Molly, you are among a very few people on Planet Earth who are receiving this message. The full message will appear on these pages at a particular moment and we urge you to be ready to read it at that time. Until then the pages will be blank except for these words of instruction.

The full message will appear on these pages, and at the same time to the others chosen to receive the message, at the moment of the vernal equinox next week. For you that will be 3:30 PM on 20 March.

There will be no further announcements of the message, and there will be no dramatic event at that moment. But at exactly 3:30 PM next Sunday the message will appear on your pages and on computer screens or in other forms in other places on the planet. Please read it then and act accordingly.

We will tell you now that your lives will be radically changed. We believe that they will be changed for the better.

The Message ✦ Part One ✦ The Event

After talking together about it for some minutes they had decided to take it seriously and to be ready when the time came for **THE MESSAGE** to appear.

Joe and Molly had left the envelope with its six sheets of blank paper on the top of the TV, where they often left bills until they were ready to pay them and other mail they wanted to keep. It had been there now for five days along with a wedding announcement from Joe's buddy who was the last of the gang to marry, an announcement for a rock concert coming up for which they had not yet decided to spend the money, and several bills. Each of them had opened the envelope several times, but nothing new was there. Only the initial instructions and six more blank sheets of paper—blank except for a border around each page and faint lines indicating perhaps something to follow, though they simply looked to Joe like a lined notepad on which nothing had yet been written.

They still thought it might be a hoax. But Joe wondered whether it might be some sort of advertising written in invisible ink. Some sort of ink which would become visible at the time stated in the instructions. Even as late as last evening Molly had said to her husband, "Oh Joe, it's probably nothing important."

But now on the twentieth of March at nearly three-thirty in the afternoon they sat quietly with steaming cups of coffee, watching the clock on the wall, until just at 3:30 **THE MESSAGE** appeared on the sheets in Joe's hand and they read together:

WarrenHall Crain

**From:
The Collective Consciousness
of The Universe**

**To:
The chosen people of The New Earth**

We begin by assuring you that this message and the new reality to which it refers is fully for your good, though we do realize that you may question its beneficence. Please read this message carefully and take it seriously. We are who we claim to be and we have done what we have deemed best.

There are now only one billion people on your planet. You who have received this message have been chosen, each of you, for the special role you can play in The New Earth. For some of you this role will be obvious. For others, while it may at first seem obvious, you will find new and perhaps surprising places to invest your talents, education and energies. For some, your role will for some time be a mystery and you may ask in bewilderment, "Why was I chosen?"

Though we realize the intense shock which

The Message ◆ Part One ◆ The Event

this event will surely be to you, nevertheless we hope that you will soon adjust to the new reality. Seek out whatever help you need from those who remain with you. Seek strength in music or literature or meditation. You will find neither tobacco nor hard drugs, though alcoholic beverages are available (yes, Joe, there is still Foster's in the fridge). We urge you not to seek solace in heavy drinking but rather to find positive ways to move into your new lives; what one of your psychiatrists some years ago referred to as "positive addictions."

We are The Collective Consciousness of the Universe—all the thoughts of all sentient beings everywhere. We are, perhaps, what you have been seeking in your SETI projects in your Search for Extra Terrestrial Intelligence. Though in reality we are more than extra-terrestrial as we include all terrestrial intelligence as well. You are part of us.

We have taken drastic action. Not unique, but rarely used. We almost always choose to allow planetary and inter-galactic societies to grow, change, and adapt as they will with no interference from Collective Consciousness. Where, in those few instances, we have taken this drastic step of intervention it has always proved beneficial, though this is by no means assured. Your future is in your hands.

You will, of course, be asking yourselves and each other why we are taking this shattering action. We answer by quoting from one of your most perceptive religious texts. In The Bhagavad Gita Lord Krishna tells Arjuna that "whenever dharma declines and the purpose of life is forgotten I manifest myself on Earth." (Bhagavad Gita IV:7, translation by Eknath Easwaran, Nilgiri Press) Perhaps those *rishis* had a sense that we have done this before in other societies which needed our extreme help and that we probably will do this again. There is also the story of The Flood in your Bible.

Take comfort in these admittedly difficult first days of your new society—we will not arrogate to ourselves the perhaps new naming of the planet, though we might suggest at first that you simply refer to "The New Earth." We have, of course, your own best interests at heart. We <u>are</u>, indeed, your own best interests and the best interests of universal consciousness. We support you in ways

The Message ◆ Part One ◆ The Event

which are often inscrutable and seemingly unknowable, though your deepest thinkers reach some understanding of our ways and your best religious texts and traditions elucidate and illuminate our existence. We do not meddle and we will not meddle; though the very action we have now taken could be construed as a monstrous act of meddling.

One of your most perceptive men in the last century wrote these words shortly before he was taken from you by the very forces which have impelled us to our drastic action: "With all the Powers for good to stay and guide us..." We are, indeed, the "Powers for good" to which Dietrich Bonhoeffer referred in a New Year's Day poem.

To paraphrase somewhat one of your greatest political documents: When in the course of human events, it becomes necessary for a greater power to take drastic control of events, a decent respect to the opinions of humankind requires that we declare the causes which impelled us to this action.

These are the factors which have led us to do what we have done:

- Your still out-of-control population growth.
- Your continuing sullying of the very air you breathe and the water you drink. Your air should be clear and your lakes and rivers and streams and oceans clean.
- Your hankering after more and more of the things material wealth brings rather than using these things to enhance your inner life.
- The continuing abysmal state of medical care. Most of your people cannot afford or do not have available even minimal health care.
- The continuing low state of education, particularly for girl children. Most of your people cannot read.

We do realize that, given more time, you might adequately have dealt with these horrendous issues. Nevertheless, we have decided to accept no further degradation of life on your planet.

It hardly need be said that we have vast powers. We have already demonstrated that unquestionably, and in the days and weeks and months ahead you will find many other aspects of our direct action. Some that may

The Message ✦ Part One ✦ The Event

confuse or disturb you and some that will please. We have eliminated flies and mosquitoes as well as cockroaches and rats. This is one of our gifts to your ongoing goodness of life.

You will find vast areas of cities, towns, villages entirely shut down. Buildings remain there, great libraries, factories, schools, hospitals, museums. These places remain for your later exploration and use. All food and other perishable items and many excess vehicles have been removed. We suggest that you concentrate your energies for some time on the places of the living. The infrastructure for your ongoing life remains in place—electricity and communication systems, roads, railroads, airlines (though many have been eliminated), governmental services.

All that you need to continue your well-developed style of life is available in these places, though you will notice many differences. Those who are used to getting your news regularly from Doordarshan or the ABC Nightly News or the South Africa Times will have to adjust to the new realities. Though you are, of course, free to rebuild these services, if you wish. "The Hindu," published in Chennai, will continue both on paper and on line. "World News For Public Television" will continue on the Public Broadcasting System.

   We will not tell you what you must do now. That is for you to decide. We will only suggest that you seek balance in all things—what The Buddha called "The Middle Way"; that you seek a style of continuing life on Planet Earth which will ensure adequate access to all the necessary resources of the planet for every living being; that you seek a just, equitable and ecologically sustainable society. We do not know that this will happen, as you are free to design your own ongoing life. We do know, in our Collective Consciousness, that it was not happening.

   We remain abundantly hopeful and optimistic. Yours is one of the loveliest planets in the universe.

   We close by remembering a phrase by the space poet Rhysling who longed to return to "the cool green hills of Earth." Our wish for you is that you will ensure that Earth remains a planet of "cool green hills."This is the only direct communication you will receive from us.

The Message ♦ Part One ♦ The Event

Molly sat quietly with Joe for several minutes, stunned by the enormity of **THE MESSAGE**. Then crying out, "Joe, the children...." she dashed for the stairs and up to the girls' bedroom, terrified that they might not be among those chosen to remain on Earth. Flinging open their door, with Joe close behind her, she found both girls playing together quietly. Roughly, in her relief and with an intense wave of love, she caught her baby girl up in her arms, as Joe swept the older girl up in his. Six-year-old Bonnie and eight-year-old Winnie, bewildered at their parents' behavior, asked "Mum, Dad, what's happening, what's the matter?"

"Nothing. Nothing's the matter. You're here, that's all. You're here," Molly said, tears flowing down her face. "We'll explain all of this to you later. Now go back to your play." And the girls, in the safe assurance of their parents' love, went back to their dolls.

Joe and Molly slowly went back downstairs to the kitchen, immensely relieved that their children were with them. Joe remembered that night eight years before when he had held his first baby daughter there by Molly's bed in the hospital where she worked. "Let's call her 'Winsome'," Molly had said. And that was her name, though everyone now called her "Winnie." Molly was thinking about Bonnie and thanking God for this second girl.

They said nothing to each other for a long time that morning. Joe read through **THE MESSAGE** again. Molly began lunch preparations. One would have thought it an ordinary morning. Each was engrossed in thought as they began to try to make sense out of what they were just beginning to realize was an enormous new reality. Molly went back upstairs twice more just to reassure herself that the girls were really still there before she spoke.

"Joe, you don't think this is just some sort of joke, do you? How can there be only one billion people left on Earth? And if there are, then why are we four chosen? Maybe this isn't real. Maybe it's just a dream." If she had not been sure that the girls were upstairs she would have been terrified. "What should we do, Joe?"

Anyone who knew Joe knew that he was slower to respond than Molly. But they also knew that he would carefully think through his response and always seemed to be right on target. Now he answered thoughtfully, "I don't think it's a joke. But I sure don't know why we've been chosen, and I'm sure glad that the girls are with us. .... What should we do? I don't know really. If **THE MESSAGE** is real, probably the first thing is to find out who else is still here. We'll call your folks first, then mine."

"The number you have reached is no longer in service." Both calls—to Molly's parents and to his—received this same automated response. And Joe began to realize the enormity of what people would soon call **THE EVENT.**

Apparently their parents were not among **THE CHOSEN.**

2. United States

Michael

(12:30 AM, Sunday, 20 March 2016 CE)

Michael was a tap dancer. He danced well and aspired to be a great dancer. He was a New York City boy from the South Bronx. He had had little formal dance training but had danced recently in a workshop led by Savion Glover, and Savion had urged him to keep on dancing. Michael was not well educated by the standards of Columbia University but he had street smarts. A tall, handsome nineteen year old, his skin was so dark that he had the nickname "Africa" in his African-American neighborhood, and he was always the first one chosen in a pick-up game of basketball at the court next to St. Stephen's Roman Catholic Church. He and his buddies often chatted with the priest there, though Michael and his family belonged to the New Hope Missionary Baptist Church across the street. Michael was one of **THE CHOSEN**.

Having read **THE MESSAGE** on the computer his family had recently installed in the living room, he had not noticed the disappearance of the others. There was no puff of smoke or flash of lightning such as he himself might have used on the stage for such a dramatic event. His family simply was not here.

The Message ◆ Part One ◆ The Event

Looking out the window he saw a quiet spring evening. Before **THE MESSAGE** had arrived, it had been a normal spring day. The sunset had been lovely and the breeze pleasant. But something was different, very different. It took Michael a moment to realize that, though he could hear the rustle of the curtains at the windows, he heard no traffic sounds from the street and no voices at all. Looking across at the playground at the projects he saw nobody, and looking up and down the streets he saw no movement of people or vehicles.

Nobody else was in the apartment. Only moments before, his wife had been in the kitchen cleaning up after dinner. Their seven-month-old son had been playing in a high chair near her. His Father had been watching TV right there in the same room. Michael's panic subsided a bit as he remembered that his mother had just gone to the supermarket across the street in the projects to buy some milk. Surely she would be right back. But the others were gone. **THE MESSAGE** had said that there would be some severe personal disruptions, but in these first few minutes after **THE EVENT** Michael was not ready even to begin to understand the enormity of what had happened to him.

Surely his whole family could not be gone. Surely he was not alone. He did not yet know that he was the only human being left in all of New York City. Soon enough he would realize this. Later he would wonder why he had been chosen, bewildered that **COLLECTIVE CONSCIOUSNESS** had chosen him. Much later still, many years later, as **THE NEW EARTH** reorganized, he began to see his crucial role as a dancer, indeed a spirit man who through the power of dance helped many others understand, cope with, and finally rejoice in the radically new reality in which they lived.

At this moment, in these first minutes after **THE EVENT**, Michael was badly shaken, afraid, alone, though not yet realizing how alone he was. He expected his mother to walk through the door at any moment, wondering as he did where everyone else was.

His family had not taken the initial messages very seriously, thinking perhaps that this was some advertising promotion or even some hoax or computer virus. The messages had come for several days: simply "Watch your computer screen at thirty minutes past midnight Eastern Standard Time on Sunday, March Twentieth, 2016." He learned later that **THE MESSAGE** was personalized so that each person had local time and date on his message. His father had just said, "Well now, Michael (He only called his son by his full given name when he had something very serious to say to him, usually calling him either "Mike" or "Bubba," the family's pet name for him). And now he was only feigning seriousness when he said "Well now, Michael, you jes let us know what this message business's all 'bout when you get it." Michael's wife had chuckled at the old man's attempt at seriousness.

Now they were gone. His Father and his wife—and his son. His mother had taken the preliminary messages so lightly that she had not even stayed home at the time **THE MESSAGE** was to come. So Michael

The Message ♦ Part One ♦ The Event

did not yet realize that his mother was also gone. He did not know that he was alone.

He was not entirely alone, for there were one billion others on the planet as **THE MESSAGE** had said, but he was alone in New York City. The nearest human beings, though he did not yet know this, were in Ithaca, up in the Finger Lakes region. Soon enough he would realize this, and within a few days he would himself be with them.

He was to go through a terrifying week of search, both in his world and within himself. Looking for other human beings in the world around him. And looking inside himself for the strength to survive what he was already thinking of as **THE EVENT.** Michael was strong—he had, after all, grown up in the South Bronx—and he knew that he would survive even this. In these first stock-taking moments, though, he was still expecting his mother to walk back into the apartment.

Though the TV was on in front of the chair where his Father had been sitting only moments earlier, the screen was blank. Seizing the remote Michael switched channels until he came to Channel Nine, the PBS station he often watched, and was somewhat reassured to see and hear Carol Obwana of World News for Public Television. Though it was not time for the news, nevertheless here she was. This must be the first news of **THE MESSAGE,** he thought. As he watched and listened Michael realized that even this suave, urbane newscaster seemed shook as she began both to comprehend the magnitude of **THE EVENT** and to help others who were still alive on the planet start to cope with **THE NEW REALITY:**

> *This is Carol Obwana broadcasting from the BBC in London with a special edition of World News for Public Television.*
>
> *Just a few minutes ago, at the exact moment of the beginning of spring, a message was received, apparently by every human being still alive on the planet. We in the studio are trying to put the details together in order to give you a coherent account of what has happened. We will be updating this bulletin often as we research the situation. Please stay tuned to this channel. Apparently the other channels are not broadcasting. Here is what we know now.*
>
> *For the past several days individuals and organizations have been receiving messages on their computer screens, by e-mail, by voice-mail, by international post, and in some cases in remote areas by special messenger. We've been reporting on these messages which have simply instructed people to watch for a major announcement at the time of the vernal equinox. What we are now calling* **THE MESSAGE** *was received just twelve minutes ago. Here is a summary by our political*

The Message ◆ Part One ◆ The Event

analyst, Gordon Blair:

> *This is Gordon Blair with World News for Public Television.*
>
> *A few minutes ago a message was received, purportedly from The Collective Consciousness of The Universe, stating in essence that the state of this planet had deteriorated so badly that Collective Consciousness has in one swift stroke brought earth's population of more than seven billion people down to a mere one billion. We here in the studio and you listening are among* **THE CHOSEN.** *Reports are beginning to come in which seem to be substantiating that something of monumental significance has taken place. We are not yet ready to believe that there are only one billion human beings left alive on the planet, but surely many, many people who were with us a few minutes ago are simply not here. Many of you who are watching know this first hand in your own homes.*
>
> *We will continue our research and will report as we know more.*
>
> *This is Gordon Blair in London.*

And this is Carol Obwana again. As Gordon has reported, it seems that **THE MESSAGE** *is in fact just what it purports to be. We are receiving many substantiating details and at this time have no reason to believe that this is a hoax. We will keep updating this story. But right now we believe that* **THE MESSAGE** *is just what it says it is.*

If this is so, as we believe it is, this is a cataclysmic event in human history. The reality of our continuing life on this planet is so radically different that we might now begin seeing ourselves as citizens of **THE NEW EARTH.**

This is Carol Obwana with World News for Public Television.

Michael turned from the TV with a feeling of relief that what seemed to be happening to him was not an isolated situation for a young man in the South Bronx but seemed to be the situation around the world. This feeling, though, was mixed with dread and confusion as he began to realize that his life had in one swift stroke been radically changed. He left the TV on and walked out of the apartment onto the sidewalk below.

Looking up and down a sidewalk usually filled with people even at midnight, and out into a street usually busy with cars, buses, trucks, taxis, he saw no movement . Not a single person was to be seen anywhere. No vehicles were moving, not even a police cruiser making the rounds. Indeed there were almost no vehicles around. It was reassuring to see his own old Honda Accord right where he had left it an hour ago at the curb. But there were no other vehicles at all on his side of the street. Reassuring to find that his own car had not been taken, but weird to see almost no other vehicles.

He looked across into the projects, and could see no movement of people in any of the windows. No drug deals being made on the corner. No homeless men slumped against the building beside the dumpster. There seemed to be nobody around. He dashed across the empty street to the little supermarket in the projects hoping, yes expecting, to find his mother there buying the milk. The door opened as he approached, but inside there was nobody. His mother was not there. Nobody was there. And, stranger still, the shelves were mostly bare. There seemed to be no food at all in the store. This frightened Michael more even than his father's and his wife's and his son's disappearance. More than not finding his mother. The apparent disappearance of all the food in the supermarket meant that this event was more than a personal thing for Michael. This affected everybody.

Dashing back into the apartment, he could not bring himself to sit in his Father's chair in front of the TV but pulled up a chair from the dining table and watched as Carol Obwana again told what was known about **THE EVENT.** Surprisingly there was little more than in her initial broadcast, though she spoke with a firmer voice as if she knew that what she was saying had in fact taken place. Analysts in the studio with powerful computer help were confident now that somehow the population of earth had been instantaneously reduced to a mere one billion. There were no reports of violence. All seemed calm. Most people, including those in the studio, were in a state of initial shock.

THE SECRETARY GENERAL of THE UNITED NATIONS, from Geneva, then came on to reassure the people of earth that THE UNITED NATIONS was still functioning, though there seemed to be little contact with national governments. "At this point in the new reality which we are already calling **THE NEW EARTH**," he said, "THE UNITED NATIONS will be the government in power and earth will be policed by THE UNITED NATIONS security force." He urged people to remain calm and to stay tuned to the Public Television station which they were now watching.

Michael went back to his computer and now printed out **THE MESSAGE** so that he could carry it with him to refer to later. Some lines stood out as he reread:

— *Seek out whatever help you need, from others who remain with you....*

All well and good, Michael thought, but where are these others? His family was no longer here, there seemed to be nobody else moving in the building, and he saw not a single person on the street or in the projects across the street. Where are these others whose help I am supposed to seek?

The Message ◆Part One ◆ The Event

— *You have been chosen for the special role you can play in* **THE NEW EARTH**....

What special role? I'm just a tap dancer from the South Bronx. What special role can I possibly play in the rebuilding of society?

— **THE MESSAGE** *said a lot about this being for our own good. We do not meddle,* **THE MESSAGE** *said, and we will not meddle, though the very actions we have taken could be construed as a monstrous act of meddling....*

You goddam right, Charlie. You meddling my own family right out of my life. For my own good, you say. Who the hell are you to claim that such a monstrous act, to use your own words, is for my own good? Michael realized that his South Bronx strength was coming to his help, as it often did, in the form of anger.

And in this re-reading, after realizing that his family was no longer with him and there seemed to be nobody left even in the projects, these words stood out:

— *You will find vast areas of cities, towns, entire villages entirely shut down....*

With an ironic chuckle Michael remembered that they used to call New York a village. Perhaps this is one of the entire villages which have been shut down. And ...

— *We will not tell you what you must do now....This is the only direct communication you will receive from us.*

What the fuck are we going to do now? You fuck up our world royally and then airily say <u>we will not meddle... we will not tell you what to do ... this is the only communication....</u> You've changed our situation radically in what you yourselves call a monstrous act and now leave us to our own devices. And...

— <u>*We remain abundantly hopeful and optimistic.*</u>
That is fine for you to affirm but — What am I to do now? I'm scared, confused, alone. What am I to do now??

3. India

Chaveri

(10:00 AM, Sunday, 20 March 2016 CE)

Around the world at the very moment of the vernal equinox the message had appeared. Some read it on their computer screens, others on TV. Many received the message on paper, as Joe and Molly did. Many had received a similar mysterious envelope, identical except that the initials CC which were on Joe and Molly's envelope were in the characters of different languages, Hindi and Amharic and Russian and Arabic, and so many others.

There had been reports on the news about these mysterious messages. Most people in the world had not received any direct, personal message. And most people thought it was probably some worldwide advertising gimmick. Many were, indeed, watching the news at the time of the appearance of **THE MESSAGE**. Though those who were not among **THE CHOSEN** never received **THE MESSAGE.** They simply disappeared at the moment of **THE EVENT.**

Chaveri Mishra was one who remained.

Chaveri lived with her family in the small town of Khajuraho in central India. Khajuraho was famous for its temples and for an annual Festival of Dances which

The Message ◆ Part One ◆ The Event

drew the best dancers from all over India for a week of evening dance concerts. Chaveri wanted to be a dancer, though she was only fifteen years old. Her family had no money to pay for dance lessons and, indeed, could not afford the price of tickets to the festival. But for as along as she could remember she had cajoled the ticket takers at the festival to allow her to sneak in and stand along the back to watch the dancers. And at the festival on the year before **THE EVENT** she had boldly walked backstage at the intermission and met one of the great dancers. This dancer was so struck by Chaveri's forwardness and obvious love of the dance that she asked Chaveri to come back at the end of the evening.

Chaveri had danced that night for India's foremost Bharat Natyam dancer, who was so impressed that she made arrangements for Chaveri to begin formal dance training in Delhi. She could see that this simple village girl might one day be a great dancer.

The Khajuraho Dance Festival had been held three weeks before **THE EVENT** and Chaveri had watched it this year from back stage. She was now a student of the dancer she had met the year before.

Chaveri was at home with her family at the time of **THE EVENT.** Her father, a guard for the temple complex, mother, a home-maker, two younger sisters, several cousins from next door. In the moment **THE MESSAGE** first appeared, in Hindi, on the TV screen, most of the family disappeared. They had been there, crowded into the small back bedroom where the TV was kept. Now they simply were not there. Only Chaveri and her father and mother were among **THE CHOSEN.**

Even in their shock at the disappearance of the others they read carefully **THE MESSAGE** as it scrolled across their TV screen. Then for several long moments they sat together quietly. Chaveri's father told his wife and daughter to stay where they were while he went outside to see who else was there.

In the lane outside their house nobody was to be seen. He knocked on several doors and found nobody. This was a busy lane and usually by this time—ten in the morning—people were up and about and going about their morning activities. Now he saw nobody, though he could hear shouting from the main chowk by the temples.

Going back inside, he took Chaveri and his wife with him to join the few people who were now gathering across from the temple gates. He was reassured to find several friends among the small group of people. Chaveri, too, found some friends and classmates.

Together they began the long process of the reorganization of their lives in **THE NEW EARTH.**

4. Russia

Svetlana

(2:30 PM, Sunday, 20 March 2016 CE)

Svetlana Ivanovna was in her office. At age thirty-five, she was the youngest mayor the city of Yakutsibirsk had ever elected. From the time she had been a little girl she had been fascinated by politics. She had seen vast changes in Russia. The collapse of the communist system and the struggle to transform into a democratic society. She was an honors graduate from Yakutsibirsk University, now with a doctoral degree in political science.

At the time of **THE EVENT** she was in her office with a small group of her closest advisors. Other groups were gathered at computer screens in other offices within the City Hall. Even in these politically knowledgeable groups there was sharp divergence of opinion about the instructions to be watching their computer screens at the moment of the vernal equinox. Several thought it an advertising ploy. Others, more darkly, feared it was perhaps an announcement from the United States about a new and fearsome weapon system which would ensure the US's dominance. Svetlana, characteristically, took a wait and see stance. She expected a message of vital importance, but spent

The Message ✦ Part One ✦ The Event

no time guessing what it might be.

At the moment **THE MESSAGE** appeared only three people remained in the Mayor's office.

Svetlana, the city treasurer and the chief of police, read the message carefully, had three copies printed, and re-read thoughtfully, before anyone spoke. Svetlana, again characteristically, was the first to speak. She always grasped the import of situations more swiftly than anyone. Now realizing the enormity of the task before them she began to issue orders first to evaluate the situation and then to deal with the re-organization of her city. The media began calling her "The Mayor Guiliani of Yakutsibirsk", recalling the style of Mayor Guiliani of New York on the day of the attack on the world trade center there.

So the reorganization began around the world. In small places and large. In big cities and small towns. On farms and in villages. In homes and schools and colleges. In factories and hospitals. Everything had changed. Where there had been huge crowds of people now there were only handfuls. Indeed in many places there were no people at all. At the moment of **THE EVENT** in all five boroughs of New York City only one person remained. There were only one billion people left in all the earth, only about thirteen percent of the population an instant before.

Though many were devastated by the loss of loved ones and friends, nobody was physically hurt.

Individual reaction to **THE EVENT** varied across the spectrum of human emotion. Many cried in terror. Others were simply confused. A surprising number of people took the news calmly and began immediately to take steps to go on with their lives. As social scientists and media people and others began to try to make sense of what had happened one of the first questions asked was why these particular one billion had been chosen. There seemed to be no rational plan of choice. Except for a few people who were in positions obviously necessary for the continuance of orderly life, such as The Chief of Police and the treasurer and the mayor in Yakutsibirsk.

Otherwise it seemed almost a random choice. Collective Consciousness had rid the world of flies, mosquitoes, rats, and cockroaches. But several criminals still remained in jails around the world. Why had they remained among **THE CHOSEN**? As **THE MESSAGE** had said, some would wonder and some would discover later why they had been chosen.

In the years following **THE EVENT** the world swiftly became a place of abundance. Products and systems which were designed for a population in the billions now were available for the one billion who remained. Political and economic structures were swiftly built to enable the equitable distribution of goods and services. The arts flourished as people found they had time to attend concerts and plays. Many took up painting and sculpture and dance, using the time they had previously spent commuting to a job in the city. The languages of the world, far from melting into one world language, strengthened, as people found they had time for language classes and study.

The Message ◆Part One ◆ The Event

It seemed that the world was now utopia. The Dark Years however, which came only a few years after **THE EVENT**, proved that it was not that simple. Later, though, In The Peace of Jerusalem, a new world order was forged which finally enabled peace and an equitable distribution of the world's resources.

5. China

Tien Wei
(12:30 PAM, Sunday, 20 March 2016 CE)

My favourite professor at Beijing University was Dr. Tien Wei, a highly respected professor of political science. Not head of his department, because he was not good at the sort of academic politicking which is often necessary to move up to such high status. He was often at odds with his colleagues over differences of understanding of their academic disciplines or the world around them. But, though arguments sometimes grew fierce and tempers sometimes flared, Dr. Tien treated his colleagues with unfailing respect. Their respect in return was always deeper than the anger of some of their moments together. All who knew him admired him as a great teacher.

At forty-five he was in the prime of his career. His journal articles and other writings were widely read by political scientists around the world, and many were on required reading lists at other universities. In many places his writings foreshadowed the Nationalist/Universalist compromise which enabled The Peace of Jerusalem fifteen years later.

He was in demand as a public speaker outside of the world of academia, and within the university most of his classes were held in large lecture halls. At

The Message ◆ Part One ◆ The Event

registration I always went early to ensure my place in his classes.

His dark complexion showed at least a touch of Mongolian heritage and it was often said that his acerbic wit and confrontive arguing style came from his Wild West background. He stood not much over a metre and a half tall, small and wiry. Always impeccably dressed. Usually in a dark three-piece suit, though often in the peasant, proletarian outfit which Chairman Mao had championed in the early years of The Communist Revolution half a century earlier. Though, of course, he changed into shorts and gym shoes for afternoons at the gym, where he was known as "The Terror of the Racquetball Courts."

We students adored him, and he returned our love and respect. Though, as with his colleagues so with his students, this adoration often manifested itself in fierce conflict. Invitations to his Thursday-Evening-At-Home firesides were more precious than tickets to the most popular rock concerts or university football matches. Only ten students were invited every Thursday. Not by any means only the cream of the crop or only graduate students. He held the tickets in his pocket and, on Mondays or Tuesdays or Wednesdays, sometimes as late as his last class on Thursday, he would give them out to whoever he chose. Students of statistics had actually written papers seeking to determine the pattern of his choice. No pattern had ever been found. Professor Tien, when asked how he chose, simply answered in an inscrutable Han-Chinese way, "I choose."

On the morning of **THE EVENT** (though, of course, we were not yet calling it that as we had not yet received **THE MESSAGE**) Dr.Tien was in a large, crowded lecture hall. Though it was Sunday, every seat was taken and many students and faculty members were standing along the back and side walls. To nobody's surprise, Dr. Tien was in animated conversation not with other faculty members but with a small group of students whom he had not previously met.

Anticipation was high as we all expected some sort of political announcement. Nobody had any idea of what the announcement might be or even who it might come from. Many expected some sort of UNITED NATIONS policy statement. Others, with a touch of paranoia, feared the announcement of some terrible weapon which would change the course of history. History was, indeed, about to be changed, but in ways much more radical than anyone realised or guessed.

We had been instructed to watch TV screens at the moment of the vernal equinox. It had seemed strange, even ominous, that there had been no indication of which channel or channels to watch. So people around the world were watching whatever they chose to watch. Here in Beijing it was early afternoon. Many were watching the Noon News. Some were paying no attention, expecting to catch up on the news when they got up later. Many thought this a hoax.

The chatter of 275 people crowded into the lecture hall stilled as the moment of the equinox

The Message ♦ Part One ♦ The Event

approached. All eyes were turned toward the front of the room as words appeared on the screen. I had expected to see someone's face—a news commentator or a politician or even The UN Secretary General himself. But there were only words—Chinese on one side, English on the other. No sound.

> **Students and faculty members of Beijing University, please pay close attention to The Message which follows, and please remain calm. We cannot stress this too strongly. Please remain calm.**
>
> **A cataclysmic event is about to take place on your planet, an event which will at first be disorienting and difficult for you.**
>
> **After a few minutes to calm yourselves we will give you a message which will explain what has happened.**
>
> **Please remain calm.**

The screen again went blank and, in an instant, in the blinking of an eye, 236 people simply disappeared. There was no noise, no flash of light or puff of smoke. But in a room which a moment before had been crowded now only 39 people remained. It was only after **THE MESSAGE** had appeared, only after those few of us who remained had read it, only after we had begun to catch our breath, that some few mathematically inclined students realised that we were in fact a group of great privilege. The population of Planet Earth—if they could believe **THE MESSAGE**—had been reduced to only one billion, less than fifteen per-cent of the previous population. In this lecture hall about seventeen percent were still here. We were, indeed, a group of high privilege.

Conversations quickly sprang up as we reached out to the few others around us to begin trying to make some sense of this incomprehensible event.

My first reaction was terror as I realised that though I was among **THE CHOSEN** my best friend was not. Only moments before he had been sitting next to me. Now there was only an empty seat. Charlie was not there. His notepad and pen were gone. His jacket, which had been flung across the back of his seat, was gone. Others in the room were filled with the same terror, and panic was close to breaking out. The hall might well have erupted into chaos had our favourite teacher not been one of **THE CHOSEN.**

Professor Tien strode to the front of the room and, acting as if this were an ordinary (though that word was rarely applicable to his class sessions) lecture, simply called for us to take our seats and be quiet. "Let's see whether we can get hard copies of **THE MESSAGE",** he said, pushing a few buttons on the equipment recently installed in this lecture hall.

In a few minutes thirty-nine copies of **THE MESSAGE** appeared in the delivery tray of the printer at the side of the room. A professor sitting on that side

The Message ◆ Part One ◆ The Event

distributed them and Professor Tien began the seminar.

Strange. We had all just experienced an event unprecedented in history and our favourite professor launched into what seemed like a seminar with what for him was an unusually small group of students. He treated **THE MESSAGE** as if it was a journal article which he wanted us to discuss. Looking back on that day I realize that he performed a marvellous service for us, helping us to begin the process of understanding **THE EVENT**.

"Let's take it from the top," he began. "I think that we can at the very least assume that **THE MESSAGE** is not a hoax. Most of the people who were crowding into this room minutes ago are simply not here." And then, though he rarely resorted to humour in his teaching, Professor Tien remarked, "It sometimes happens that one or two sneak out of my lectures, but never a mass exodus like this. How many of us remain?"

"39," answered someone, "of the 275 who were here before. I counted."

"Let's see, that must be about ten percent."

"No, it is about seventeen percent."

"It seems then," continued Professor Tien, "that we are among the privileged few chosen to remain. As **THE MESSAGE** states, each of us was chosen for the special role we can play on earth. Our most important task over the next few days and weeks will be to begin discerning that task. I suggest that in a few minutes we dismiss this seminar and each of us as a homework assignment carefully re-read **THE MESSAGE** and write a brief essay answering three questions:

1. Why am I here? Why am I personally among **THE CHOSEN?**
2. What are the major challenges/tasks facing me/us in this coming year?
3. Given the new population reality what is your vision for Planet Earth?

We will re-convene in this room tomorrow morning at nine. Now I know that each one of us has enormous personal tasks ahead of us as we begin to deal with this event. I close today's seminar by pointing out that the authors of **THE MESSAGE** at one point referred to themselves as 'All the powers for good.' I remind you that those powers have pledged to <u>support us in ways which are often inscrutable and unknowable.</u> I believe that, as **THE MESSAGE** said, <u>this is for the good.</u>"

"Chong, will you stay with me for a moment?" Tien Wei spoke to his colleague and dear friend, life-long bachelor and chairperson of the chemistry department. "Do you have your mobile with you?" Professor Chong reached into his briefcase and handed Tien Wei his phone. With trembling hands, barely able to contain his apprehension, fearing the answer, Tien Wei dialed his wife's personal number.

"This is a message from collective consciousness. The person whose number you reached is no longer with Earth's people." Only that brief, blunt announcement. No softening. Tien Wei's analytical, scientific mind realized that millions around the world must be hearing this same message as they tried to reach wives, husbands, lovers, friends.

The Message ♦Part One ♦ The Event

But now, class having been dismissed, in the lecture hall empty except for himself and his friend, bereft, his face distorted with grief, with tears welling up in his eyes and anguish in his voice, Tien Wei reached out and grasped Chong's hands tightly, "She's gone, Chong. Su Ling is gone."

II.

THE DARK YEARS

2026–2031 CE

1. Assassination of Carol Obwana
(1 January 2026 CE)

"OH GOD!" SHE cried, as shots rang out in the studio. And with these words, which echoed Mahatma Gandhi's last words seventy-eight years earlier, the anchor person on "World News for Public Television" slumped across her desk and died. Television screens around the world went blank for several minutes. Then General Amir Muhammad's face came on.

General Amir had been active for many years in the ongoing struggles between Pakistan and India and was well known now as the head of The Nationalist Movement in **THE NEW EARTH**. Many people had resisted the reorganisation of the earth into nine geo-social spheres and thirty-six political districts. Many, seeing that move as an old, outmoded soviet pattern, would have preferred retaining old national identities. The movement to revert to an older political organisation on national lines had grown strong.

Now on New Year's Day ten years after **THE EVENT** The Nationalist Movement had seized power. "People of The United Nations," General Amir began, carefully choosing to refer to 'The United Nations' rather than '**THE NEW EARTH**.'

"We urge you to remain calm. Nationalist forces are

The Message ◆ Part One ◆ The Dark Years

in charge now. We have taken control of **NEW EARTH** headquarters in Geneva and of each of the district capitals. We have done this without a single shot and completely without loss of life or injury. Except, of course, the death you have all witnessed here.

"We are not desperate. But we are determined. We are in control of the system and the infrastructure of political power. We hold the allegiance of many of you, though not yet the majority. We believe that we will demonstrate to all the wisdom of our movement and that, when democratic elections are once again held, we will win your allegiance. We are determined to succeed.

"We believe that politically untenable and dangerous decisions were made in the first years after **THE EVENT**. The most basic of those decisions has brought on a malaise which is growing around the world. This decision has undermined people's pride in who they are. It has weakened cultural and humanitarian institutions. If allowed to continue, this most basic decision would emasculate us and leave us weak. I refer to the decision to repudiate national identities and reorganise on the soviet pattern artificially put together by social scientists and bureaucrats.

"That decision is now reversed. We are now once again a world of nations united in peace and moving toward a world in which every human being is free to choose her own destiny, his own path. A world in which pride in one's own nation will lead to peace and harmony among the nations.

"Within the next two years national elections will be

held enabling the people of each nation to choose their own elected officials. Until then martial law will prevail under The United Nations police forces.

"There has been only one death in this swift takeover of world power. We believe that the transition can be bloodless. We are determined to ensure that resort to physical force is avoided. Nevertheless, we are in control and we will use whatever force we deem necessary.

"This explains the death in this very studio only minutes ago. The death of a person known more widely even than I am. We are not terrorists. We chose to use this one terrorist act to underscore our determination to use whatever means are necessary to move away from a soviet style of world government to a nationalist style.

"We will prevail. You need no longer try to build enthusiasm for District 31 or District 17 or whichever of these arbitrary districts happens to be yours. Now, once again, pride in your nation and in the richness of its unique culture can move you to shout *'viva españa'*, *'bharat mata ki jai', nippon banzai'*, 'God bless America', *'swaziland uhuru'*, 'Rule Brittania'. Together we join hands as people of the many nations to go forward united toward a bright future for **THE NEW EARTH**."

Tien wei sat stunned. Almost as stunned as on that early morning in a lecture hall in Beijing ten years before when he first read **THE MESSAGE**. He had known, of course, that there had been strong opposition to the new constitution in many parts of the world. Indeed, as an eminent political scientist and as a delegate to both the first and the second constitutional conventions, he had worked tirelessly to help the world's people reach consensus on the proposed new organisation. He knew well that many objected to the new sphere and district structure and the obscuring of national boundaries. And though he was committed to the new structure as delineated in the proposed new constitution, He still thought of himself as Chinese. And he had not joined The Nationalist Movement, though he found much there to which he was drawn. In his own quiet, thoughtful way he had turned from a movement in which he found seeds of division and mistrust leading perhaps to hatred and violence. And the murder which he had just witnessed seemed to bear out his fears.

 It did not work out as General Amir had hoped. He was so fixed in his determination to remould **THE NEW EARTH** along nationalist lines that he was unable to look rationally at the immensity of the task which The Nationalists had set. The Nationalist Movement finally crumbled before the overwhelming consensus that **THE NEW EARTH** required a New Polity, one more clearly focused on the sphere and district model specified in the proposed constitution. Though the champions of the initial proposed constitution also found the need to compromise.

 Consensus was not easily reached. It grew out of immense struggle. We went through a period of turmoil which we now call "The Dark Years." General Amir, as head of government through this period, and other nationalist leaders, continued to champion the nationalist cause. Other, more thoughtful and forward looking visionaries such as Tien Wei and Svetlana Ivanovna, the mayor of Yakutsibirsk, finally prevailed in the enormously complex compromise which resulted in the adoption of the constitution and The Peace of Jerusalem.

2. Marriage of Winnie and Bonnie
(6 December 2029 CE)

It was the social event of the season in Wagga Wagga. Winnie and Bonnie had been so close as sisters that many people thought them twins, though they were two years apart in age. **THE EVENT** had brought them even closer. So nobody was surprised when they announced their marriage as a single event. A late fall Saturday afternoon wedding at the Methodist church where their family had been members since before they had been born. Their parents were leading members of the church, though neither held elected office there. It had been a difficult task to pare the guest list down to the number of people who could fit into the church sanctuary. And nearly a thousand had come to the reception later.

The grooms, too, were like brothers, though they came from widely separated parts of Earth. They were fraternity brothers whom the girls had met at university. Both tall and slim. And, of course, handsome. Active in sports. Excellent scholars, as the girls were. One was so dark that he boasted of being the darkest person in Wagga Wagga. And though some challenged him on that boast, nobody had yet been found with darker skin. The other was fair and blonde. Perhaps not the lightest skinned person in town, but certainly among the lightest. Except for their skin tone, though, these boys might also have been mistaken for twins.

Each couple had met when Winnie was a senior at the University of Wagga Wagga. Bonnie was a sophomore. And though they knew very soon that they would marry they had decided to postpone the wedding until after Bonnie's graduation. During those two and a half years the four of them were often together, preferring to go places as a foursome rather than each couple going separately. Now the wedding was as a foursome.

Joe and Molly were among the few who remained in Wagga Wagga after **THE EVENT**. And they seemed not to have changed, though **THE EVENT** changed many lives drastically all around the world. For the Lambkins life seemed to go on almost as if nothing had happened. Their family was together, just the two adults and the two girls. Many knew them as an ideal family. Joe still held his job as a custodian at the high school, and Molly was still at the City Hospital, where she was now head nurse. Everyone in town seemed to know them.

Wagga Wagga had changed. In **THE EVENT** the population had dropped from over 40,000 to under 5,000. Not as severe a drop as in many other places around the globe. There had been several years of sometimes chaotic reorganization, but in many ways the town remained the same friendly small town it had been. The major change was the influx of people from around the world. As travel had become easier and affordable to all, many people began choosing to move to other locations. And now Wagga Wagga was a very cosmopolitan, international small town. Population just under 10,000, and perhaps now stabilizing at about that number. Wagga Wagga boasted a superb university, a world-renowned symphony orchestra, and several splendid theaters. Its parks and open spaces made it a very pleasant place and life was very pleasant there.

The struggle between The Nationalists and The Universalists had not yet been resolved, but global politics seemed to have little effect here in small town Australia. Though, of course, everyone recognized that **THE NEW EARTH** was vastly different than Earth before **THE EVENT.** Many were still grieving the loss of friends and loved ones. It would take many more years, indeed several generations, for full healing of this trauma. The Lambkins, though they had not lost any immediate family member, had lost many friends and other more distant relatives, including both sets of parents.

But for Winnie and Bonnie and their two new husbands—one dark and one fair—life was beginning in their new families. Joe came down the aisle between his two daughters and stood between them as the minister asked, "Who blesses this marriage between these women and these men?" And Molly was pleased when Joe answered, "Her mother and I do." Placing Winnie's hand in her groom's dark hand and Bonnie's hand in her groom's light hand, Joe took his seat with Molly, beaming with pride and pleasure.

The Message ◆Part One ◆ The Dark Years

The ceremony, mostly very traditional, ended with the two couples kissing, but then walking together not as two couples but as a foursome, arm in arm down the aisle.

The reception, at a large hall rented just for large gatherings, was boisterous and friendly. Champagne flowed freely, and, of course, Foster's Beer. There was plenty of food for all. The bouquets were tossed by the brides, and caught by girls who blushed at the thought that they now were supposed to be the next to marry. The grooms threw their brides' garters. The wedding cake was cut—four hands on the knife. Rice was thrown as the four dashed out to their limousine—only one limo, but the longest in town. And the wedding was over.

3. The Peace of Jerusalem

(1 July 2031 CE)

Though General Amir, in seizing power, had proclaimed his victory a bloodless coup, except for the dramatic assassination of Carol Obwana on public television, sporadic violence continued as it had in the years before **THE EVENT.** But these attacks were different now. They were obviously carried out by Nationalists. And many were in the same areas which had, around the turn of the millennium, been so violent—Israel and Kashmir and Ireland and central Africa. Yet this terrorist activity was different. Perhaps it was simply because there were far fewer people now on the planet. Or because the vastly reduced population had heightened people's feelings for the value of each individual human life. The attacks now in the years after **THE EVENT** only rarely involved death or injury. They were almost always highly symbolic, involving government buildings or public places.

Some were devastating, as the bringing down of The United Nations building in 2024 CE. Though there were no suicide airliners involved, this was an attack eerily reminiscent of the bringing down of The World Trade Center twenty-three years earlier, fifteen years before **THE EVENT.** This attack was a master stroke of sabotage by The Nationalists. Warnings were given to evacuate the building and only a small team of

The Message ♦ Part One ♦ The Dark Years

Universalist police was killed. This team had entered the building in a desperate race to prevent the destruction. They died in the implosion.

Though the Nationalists had proclaimed that they were in charge, the reality was that the Nationalist forces had effectively seized control of the capital at Geneva and swiftly gained control of the rest of Europe and Africa, while the remainder of the world stayed in the control of the Universalists. The Universalist government, the United Nations, moved back to their old headquarters at the United Nations building in New York, and when that building was destroyed, easily moved to the New York State buildings in Albany only 260 km. away.

Throughout The Dark Years, as we came to call the period between the seizure of control by the Nationalists and the Peace of Jerusalem, these two governments held power, each over a portion of the earth. There were many shifts in the situation as local governments and regions changed their allegiances. And within each of the two political spheres many wished that their government was the other one.

There were numerous protests and demonstrations in the streets of the cities. Editorials in the world press argued vociferously for one side or the other. And there were still armed confrontations in many places. The Line of Control through Kashmir continued to be a hot spot, as the Nationalists held Pakistan and Afghanistan while the Universalists held China and India. A few shots were fired. But no lives were lost in that area. Indeed, very few lives were lost anywhere in the world on either side: Carol Obwana at the beginning of The Dark Years and the six Universalist police who died in the implosion of the United Nations building toward the end of that ten year period, and a very few others in other skirmishes.

The attack on the United Nations building was the last and most dramatic act of the Nationalist forces. Conferences were being held between leaders of the Nationalists and leaders of the New Earth government. Professor Tien Wei, the eminent political science professor from Beijing, had become the chosen chairman and convenor of these conferences. Revered and respected by all, Nationalist and Universalist alike, Tien Wei was clearly The Man of The Hour. Those students who had been with him there at Beijing University at the first reading of **THE MESSAGE** were by no means surprised. They recalled his calmly assigning a careful study of **THE MESSAGE** as homework that day. They now saw this same carefully targeted coolness leading, as it ultimately did, to The Peace of Jerusalem.

Svetlana Ivanovna, Mayor of Yakutsibirsk, matched Tien Wei's coolness. Though it was often obvious that her propensity was toward the Universalist side where Tien Wei's often was toward the Nationalists. Tien Wei had noticed her in the conferences. He was drawn to her openness and forthright argumentative style. She was a stolid Russian. Passionate about people, a lover of her own country yet committed to a new earth. She and Tien Wei soon found themselves in conversations around the edges of these conferences. Though they were usually at odds in the meetings they seemed to share a personal bond. She, too, had lost her partner in **THE EVENT.**

The issues had been clear. The New Earth Government, soon after **The Event** had attempted to impose a new geo-social political structure, reminiscent of old soviet style governmental planning. **THE NEW EARTH** was to be divided into three sectors -- EAST, WEST, SOUTH -- with each sector divided into three spheres and each sphere again divided into regions.

This brought a huge upwelling of nationalist fervor. Many people wanted still to be identified with their own nations. The vast majority of Americans resented the new structure and rejected the idea that they were now citizens of WEST Sector 4. They wanted to be "Americans." Palestinians wanted to be "Palestinians". The people of Kashmir wanted to be known as "Kashmiris." Even the very few people left in Iceland shunned the idea of being identified in what they saw as an arbitrary and artificial and imposed structure. They were proud to be "Icelanders."

A lasting peace ultimately grew out of the work of the final Nationalist/Universalist conference. This peace came to be known as The Peace of Jerusalem because that decisive conference was held in that city which had throughout its history been enmeshed in political controversy and violence. Delegates there in Jerusalem drew up a plan which was then ratified by all the nations of **THE NEW EARTH.**

Consensus had not been easily reached. It grew out

of immense struggle. Throughout the Dark Years civil wars raged large, though largely in diplomatic arenas and with few lives lost. The War of The Dark Years was fought almost entirely in negotiations. Often difficult. Often angry. Often severely frustrating. Almost always long and tiring. Tien Wei and Svetlana fought through these years, often at odds with each other, but always with respect. General Amir, as head of the Nationalist government through this period, with other Nationalist leaders, continued to champion the Nationalist cause. Other more thoughtful and forward looking visionaries, such as Tien Wei and Svetlana, finally prevailed. An enormously complex compromise brought about The Peace of Jerusalem.

The plan was elegant in its simplicity. National political boundaries were retained much as they had developed over the centuries. Though difficult compromises had to be made in many places such as Palestine, Kashmir, and Rwanda. The nations were now to be organized into larger economic units much as the European Economic Community had been established in the years before **THE EVENT.** A New Constitution was drawn up in later conferences and subsequently ratified by the parliaments and assemblies of the various nations of **THE NEW EARTH.**

General Amir was recognized as a world hero, respected for the honorable way in which he had led the Nationalist forces in their struggle to preserve national pride around the world. His forces were now integrated into The New Earth Police Force. And

The Message ♦Part One ♦ The Dark Years

General Amir himself was chosen as Commander of Police Forces. Svetlana and Ten Wei were honored for their role in bringing peace to the world.

The global struggle which has now been resolved in The Peace of Jerusalem had been so intense that many termed it World War III. This war, though, had been fought almost entirely in the hearts and minds of the people and in sometimes seemingly interminable political conferences, with very little loss of life or physical injury. The assassination of Carol Obwana and the bringing down of The United Nations building stood out as exceptions. Now in The Peace of Jerusalem the people of **THE NEW EARTH** hoped that a lasting peace had been achieved.

III.

THE NEW EARTH

1. The State of the New Earth Address
(1 July 2032 CE)

"Ladies and gentlemen, please welcome the Prime Minister of **NEW EARTH**."

Svetlana Ivanovna stepped to the podium to a standing ovation of both Houses of Parliament. She was to be often interrupted by applause and several points in her address brought the members to their feet. There seemed to be none of the dissension which had often rocked the Parliament, particularly in the early years after **THE EVENT**. This address was to be a joyous report on the advances which had been made on many fronts and the splendid state of **THE NEW EARTH.**

"Ladies and gentlemen, and children of **THE NEW EARTH,**" Svetlana began, realizing that most people in the world were tuned in to the television broadcast of this address. "Ladies and Gentlemen, and Children of **THE NEW EARTH**, it is a privilege to report to you this evening on the state of our planet and of human society around this world and in our first outposts beyond Earth. All is well for humanity.

"I will not dwell on the past, the first years of struggle to reorganize human society after **THE**

The Message ◆Part One ◆ The New Earth

EVENT. I will not dwell on the events of the Dark Years and the battles between the Nationalists and the Universalists, except to express my gratitude to all who were involved that those battles were fought largely in these very halls and in other meeting places like this and few lives were lost. I will not dwell on the consensus which was forged in The Peace of Jerusalem, except to say that the peace which we found then seems to be a lasting one.

"I will this evening point to evidences in ten arenas which demonstrate that human society on this planet is alive and well. I begin with the economy, medical care, education, and housing.

"The economic life of **THE NEW EARTH** is strong. With our six global currencies, the dollar, the euro, the rand, the ruble, the rupee, and the yuan, every person has adequate income. But the greed of the past which threatened to swamp the earth in more and more goods seems to be in the past. Most people are leading simpler lives. And the gap between the rich and the poor which has plagued our world for so long is now no longer a problem. Nobody is living any longer in abject poverty and nobody is living with extreme wealth.

"Medical care is now free for all citizens of **THE NEW EARTH,** and the freedom and necessary funds to pursue medical research without the burden of overstressed facilities has enabled some phenomenal breakthroughs. Though we are still a long way from conquering cancer we have made great strides in the treatment of HIV-AIDS and are close to a cure.

"Basic education, too, through college and graduate schools for those who wish to pursue higher education, is seen as a birthright and is available at no cost to all citizens. Many are pursuing degrees in a wide range of fields. One example, one which has surprised many of us, is the strengthening of the world's languages. Many social scientists had feared that we would be moving swiftly toward one global language. What we have discovered, however, is that people are freed from the demands of working long hours and many are perfecting their linguistic abilities. There are marvelous computer aided learning systems in every known world language. Choose your language and learn to read it and write it and speak it. Few citizens there are who speak less than two or three languages.

"Before **THE EVENT** every country of the world was struggling with the problem of homelessness. People were sleeping on the streets and sidewalks of almost every major city and millions more were living in slums. "A roof over every bed" became a slogan of those working to end homelessness, but the challenge was immense. Now, with Earth's vastly reduced population, everyone has a safe and secure place in which to sleep in a rich variety of houses and housing styles. Of course, in India in the hot season, many still prefer to sleep up on the roof with a roof <u>under</u> the bed.

"Three other arenas to which I will point to

The Message • Part One • The New Earth

demonstrate that human society on **THE NEW EARTH** is alive and well are technology, travel and our move into space.

"One sees everywhere advances and breakthroughs in technology. I will point to only a few. Around the world now the air is nearly back to the pristine cleanliness which it had up until the last half of the 20th century of the common era. This is due in large part to advances in automotive technology which were simply being outpaced by runaway population growth. Now, we have also perfected engines which burn hydrogen and whose exhaust is cleaner than the intake air. Our electricity is produced totally by non-polluting sources -- wind and solar primarily. In the field of medical care breakthroughs in micro-robotics are healing and curing and preventing further damage, easing pain and bringing health. Our lives are touched every day by new technologies which were not even dreamed about twenty-five years ago.

"Two factors have spurred a huge burst in global travel. The hypersonic airliner now makes travel between almost any two cities in the world so short that cabin staff hardly have time to serve a decent meal before the captain announces the descent into the destination airport. Vastly increased discretionary income allows people to choose to travel where and when they choose, and many do so. On business or pleasure. And often with the whole family or groups of friends. This has been an incentive to the growth of linguistic ability which I spoke about earlier.

"Space exploration proceeds apace. Sixty-four years ago the great film-maker, Stanley Kubrick, produced the film 2001AD. Now, thirty-one years after 2001AD, we have a city on the moon and a colony on Mars. And political and scientific debate rages about the advisability or non-advisability of terra-forming Mars. Many believe that in less than 500 years the surface of Mars could be made habitable by human beings, with breathable atmosphere. Others propose that we protect the Martian environment, and live in colonies under the surface or under glass surface domes. We are pushing exploration toward the edges of the known universe, though astro-physicists still have little understanding of either the birth or the extent of the universe.

"Three other arenas to which I will point to demonstrate that human society on **THE NEW EARTH** is alive and well are the environment, the arts, and peace.

"Our natural environment on earth was under severe strain—one might better use the word "assault" at the turn of the millennium. Indeed, it was this assault—on the world's forests and its rivers and streams, on the oceans, on pristine places such as the Arctic National Wildlife Refuge and the continent of Antarctic—it was this assault which was a major impetus to Collective Consciousness in bringing about **THE EVENT.** Now vast areas of **THE**

The Message ◆ Part One ◆ The New Earth

NEW EARTH have been set aside as World Wildlife Refuges, including the Kanha National Park in India where perhaps slightly over one hundred tigers lived. This National Park has been extended to include most of the sub-continent from the Tropic of Cancer to beyond Sri Lanka. The tiger population—one of the world's foremost indicators of the health of natural forest ecology—is expanding rapidly. The Brazilian Rainforest is now protected as a World Wildlife Refuge. And every country and region is increasing its national and regional park systems. Yes, Earth is alive and well.

"The arts are flourishing. This again is a function of adequate income which enables leisure time. The phenomenal work of The Ithaca Dance Theater in the beautiful finger lakes region of New York state is one evidence of the vitality of the arts. And new and classic operas performed in the stunning Sydney Opera House. Painting and sculpture in Beijing. Weaving in Nairobi. Literature and drama pouring out of the minds of people everywhere, some still writing with fountain pens of a previous era, others using more up-to-date technology. And the movies. Bollywood and Hollywood still vie for supremacy, though now other film capitals are producing some amazing films. Interestingly, we still call them films, though almost all are now totally digital, with no film involved at all.

"And FINALLY, PEACE. FINALLY, PEACE. FINALLY, PEACE. **THE NEW EARTH** is a world at peace. Peace protected by a global police force under the command of our dear friend General Amir Muhammad. War and rumors of war raged large over the earth and only a few short years ago the world's people lived in the fear of weapons of mass destruction being unleashed at any time. These have now been destroyed and will never again bring such terror to humankind. WE ARE A WORLD AT PEACE.

"It has been my privilege this evening to address you all, citizens of **THE NEW EARTH.** To assure you that all is well and to wish you all the very best in the years to come.

Svetlana Ivanovna
1 July 2032

IV.

DANCING IN THE NEW EARTH

THE KHAJURAHO DANCE FESTIVAL

1. Michael and Chaveri

(21 March 2033 CE)

Flashes of lightning, moving off to the Southwest, fill the sky behind the temples. The sky above is brilliant with stars and a waxing quarter moon hangs over the newly build Khajuraho Dance Pavilion. Not only is this the sixtieth anniversary of the annual dance festival; it is also the dedication of the new Temple of the Peoples. Tonight a sold out amphitheatre waits expectantly to welcome my dear friends Chaveri and Michael, the wife-and-husband team famous for fusion of eastern and western dance styles.

 The night is warm, as it always is here on the days of the dance festival. The audience, festively dressed and from most of the nations of **THE NEW EARTH**, chats quietly as the musicians tune.

 The stage is a starkly simple vast stone platform. A line of slender doric columns sets it off from the backdrop of two magnificent temples—one a thousand years old, the other brand new. The musicians – playing sitar, rock-guitar, tabla, bongo drums, harmonium, keyboard, string bass—are seated on stage right. In a soft light, seeming only to enhance the light

The Message ◆Part One ◆ Dancing in the New Earth

of the quarter moon, the temples loom over us. The stage is dark. Subdued spotlights are on the ancient *murti* of Lord Ganesha which had been brought here several days ago and newly installed here. Twenty-seven stone steps, stretching in a straight line right from one side to the other lead up to the stage. From my seat in the amphitheatre it looks as if one could simply ascend those steps, cross the stage, and walk between the columns right up to the temples, though in reality there is a substantial distance between stage and temples. I am filled with awe at the splendour of the night sky, the magnificence of these temples old and new, the stark elegance of this new amphitheatre and the anticipation of tonight's performance.

The musicians finish tuning and the audience comes to a hush as new, brilliant spotlights pick out the two dancers at the top of the centre aisle behind the audience.

Chaveri's deep rose *sari* sets off her dark beauty. Michael, darker and taller, is handsome beside her dressed in the blue jeans and white t-shirt of his rap-tap-rock dance style. He acknowledges the huge welcoming applause with a quick tap riff, picked up not by the guitar but by the sitar in a clue that this will be a marvellous evening of fusion dance and music.

As the applause quiets Michael begins to dance. His shoes tap out a complex rhythm, accompanied now by both sitar and guitar, as he moves down the aisle toward the stage. Chaveri follows, walking quietly a few steps behind her husband, head down in the role of the traditional wife. At row eight they pause and together bow and touch the feet of Chaveri's parents in reverence. I am sitting also in that row and, catching my eye, Chaveri chuckles, filled with the joy of dancing tonight with her beloved Michael.

The musicians stop playing. Michael stops dancing. All is quiet as the two dancers pause at the bottom step to remove their shoes in honour of the sacred space of the stage and the temples behind. Spotlights stay on them as, together now, hand-in-hand, they slowly ascend the steps, turning to the left to walk over to the statue of Ganesha. Touching Ganesha's feet in reverence they implore His blessing not only on their dancing this evening, but on the magnificent new temple being dedicated and on the glorious society of **THE NEW EARTH**, still very much in its infancy, only eighteen years old.

Coming now to centre stage, with joined palms they make their *namaste* to the musicians and then to the audience. Floodlights come up slowly on the temples until they are bathed in a brilliance so that all else is dark except the two temples and the two dancers.

Then, in what must surely have come from a spontaneous impulse which never would have occurred in Chaveri's traditional Bharat Natyam dance, though it would have been appropriate at Michael's Ithaca Dance Theater, these two world famous dancers, wife and husband, embrace and kiss. Laughter and applause break out as the audience signifies its pleasure and approval.

They turn then to the audience, and Michael speaks,

The Message ◆ Part One ◆ Dancing in the New Earth

"Ladies and gentlemen, we are honoured this evening to have in our presence two of the most famous people on earth. May I ask that they join us for a moment on stage. New Earth Prime Minister Svetlana Ivanovna and Professor Tien Wei."

More applause breaks out as these two people, perhaps the two people who had been most influential in bringing about The Peace of Jerusalem, come on stage. Then, these two world leaders standing between the two world famous dancers, Michael again speaks,

"It gives me great pleasure to announce that Prime Minister Svetlana and Professor Tien are now husband and wife."

This, of course, brings another embrace and kiss before Svetlana and Tien Wei resume their seats to the tumultuous applause of the audience.

Michael then moves back out of the spotlight to lean against a column to watch his wife dance. The music is now only on Indian instruments as Chaveri dances an invocation in Bharat Natyam style honouring Lord Ganesha.

While Chaveri was dancing Michael had left the stage and now a spotlight finds him on stage left, dressed in a simple white *khadi kurta-pyjama,* his face painted blue and carrying a flute, coming to join Chaveri. Now we know this dance will honour Radha and Krishna in their deep love. Again only the Indian instruments play and, if we did not know that Michael was a tap dancer from The Bronx, we would believe that these are both Indian dancers. We are caught up in the spell being woven by these two magnificent artists.

After intermission Chaveri and Michael do a fast tap dance honouring the strength and peace of the Muslim tradition in which Michael was raised. Honouring also the city of New York. Dressed now in blue jeans and white shirts the couple taps down the centre aisle as if they were strutting down 125th Street into the Apollo Theater. Now, of course, only the western instruments are played.

The evening closes with our dancers, now in Indian dress, portraying Lord Siva and his consort Parvati and honouring the new Siva temple where, we hope, people will worship every day for the next thousand years as they have worshipped in the old temple daily for the past thousand years. The music slows and quiets as the two dancers now side by side in centre stage turn to the two temples. These magnificent temples, now bathed in brilliant light, are now the focus of our attention. With palms joined in reverence Chaveri and Michael kneel, then prostrate themselves fully in honour of The Collective Consciousness, here in these temples honoured in the form of Lord Siva.

Kiran Verma, poet-laureate of Khajuraho, is in the audience. Chaveri had noticed that, not surprisingly, he was writing. Perhaps a poem especially for this occasion.

EPILOGUE: ALWAYS

The rain falls gently again tonight
And there is no wind.
But in the skies above Khajuraho
Great sheets of lightning and jagged forks
Announce the beauty of your dance,
Lord Shiva.

Surely you are pleased with your people.
Yet again you are dancing in the night sky.
Tonight you revel with us in this, your temple,
Honouring the people of **THE NEW EARTH**.

Rejoicing in a world where everyone has
Abundant food to eat;
Clean air to breathe;
Safe water to drink;
Where streams and rivers run pure and clear;
Where tigers roam the forests,
And great whales roam the seas;
A world in which health care is freely available to all;
Where everyone has a safe and secure home in which to live;
A world in which music and dance and the arts are flourishing;
And every person has access to superb education;
Where all people know you as the One **Collective Consciousness**,
Though we still worship you in richly diverse forms.

Often you have come to us, in outward show, Lord Shiva,
In the clash and furor of the storm,
Phir bhi hamesha hamare dil main tu nachta hai. *
Yet always in our hearts you dance.

* The last line is an English translation of the second last line.
This poem was written in Hindi

Kiran Verma
21 March 2033
at the dedication of
The Temple of The People
Annual Dance Festival
Khajuraho, India

Part Two

What, Then, Did Occur?

I.

What, Then, Did Occur?

THE EVENT did not happen. **COLLECTIVE CONSCIOUSNESS,** apparently at the last instant, pulled back from the brink and allowed Planet Earth to proceed on its own rather than taking the monstrous cataclysmic step of decimating Earth's population. I've no doubt that there were innumerable individual consciousnesses which were, to the end, militating for **THE EVENT. COLLECTIVE CONSCIOUSNESS,** however, always moves by consensus, and this must have been a remarkable exercise in consensus building.

The amazing result is that Kiran Verma's vision has been substantially realized, though not fully. It will take time for Earth's forests to regenerate and for great whales to repopulate the seas. The *Janata Mandir*, Temple of the People, has been built and was dedicated last year at the Khajuraho Dance Festival. Chaveri and Michael did dance that evening, and Tien Wei and Svetlana were there.

This is nothing less than a triumph of the human spirit and the human species. Indeed, this is a triumph for all life on Earth and for all sentient beings

The Message ✦ Part Two ✦ What, Then, Did Occur?

wheresoever. I believe that this is also a vindication of the truth that progress almost always comes from within – that the resources are available within an individual, within a society, within a planet – and that outside intervention is almost always debilitating or harmful in the long run. **COLLECTIVE CONSCIOUSNESS** in **THE MESSAGE** said as much in noting that an intervention such as **THE EVENT** is rarely made. In the case of Planet Earth in the year 2016 CE **THE EVENT** did not happen.

What, then, did occur? What were the major political, cultural, ecological, social, religious events in the world in the period from 2016 CE to the year 2033 CE? What really happened to the people we met in my utopian novella seventeen years ago? And what other significant progress has been made toward this vision?

THE LAMBKIN FAMILY:

Joe and Molly Lambkin are still happily married, still living in Wagga Wagga in the house on Smith Street. The house is seeming a bit small with their children and grandchildren and their many friends visiting often. Joe still works for the schools, though now in a managerial capacity, and Molly is still at the hospital. Winnie and Bonnie were both married in 2028 in a double ceremony—to their high school sweethearts. Winnie has twin boys now and Bonnie a daughter.

Wagga Wagga did not become a cosmopolitan international town, but is still much the same as it was in 2016: a pleasant small Australian town with a superb university and a very creditable symphony orchestra.

MICHAEL AND CHAVERI:

Michael kept that old Honda Accord for several more years. He is still happily married, though being a kid from The Bronx he and his wife have had some tumultuous arguments and several times came very near to divorce. They now have three children and are living in Ithaca, where Michael has established the Ithaca Dance Theatre which is becoming world famous for championing many international dance styles while focusing primarily on the tap dance tradition.

The dance at the Khajuraho Dance Festival last year was much as I envisioned it seventeen years ago, though Michael and Chaveri did not kiss, as they are not husband and wife. They are both superb dancers whose duet performances are much in demand around the world.

Chaveri is also married and makes her home in Khajuraho. She and her husband have bucked some strong family pressure and chosen to have no children.

TIEN WEI AND SVETLANA:

Tien Wei and Svetlana did marry, just a few months ago, after their previous spouses had died coincidentally last year. These two had been together many times at international conferences as each was passionately committed to finding ways for peace and solidarity for all the world's people. They had become close friends, though often at odds politically. They were at the Khajuraho Dance Festival last year, and Chaveri and Michael did make the first public announcement of their marriage.

Tien Wei has had a distinguished career in Political Science, and is still on the faculty there in Beijing. Svetlana for two terms now has been mayor of Yakutsibirsk, one of the new towns established in Siberia in response to Earth's population pressures (which, of course, did not suddenly disappear in **THE EVENT.**)

CAROL OBWANA:

Carol Obwana has had a distinguished career with BBC News and is recognized as one of the finest news persons today.

GENERAL AMIR MUHAMMAD:

General Amir has indeed been chosen as Commander of Police Forces. Not, however, for **NEW EARTH** forces, but for United Nations Police. General Amir rose to prominence at the time of the 2015 Kashmir earthquake because of his continuing attempts to reach across the Line of Control between his own Pakistan and his neighbor India. The rapprochement between these two bitter enemies was forged out in the decade following that disaster. The nations of South Asia over the past twenty years have increasingly recognized that national boundaries are not as significant as are larger economic units in the modern world. The South Asian Economic Community was formed, on the lines of the earlier European Union, with free and open boundaries among the South Asian nations and with a common currency, the New Rupee.

This has led to other groupings of nations into economic units, and we now have only six global currencies: the Dollar, the Euro, the Peso, the Rand, the Rupee, and the Yuan. The values of these fluctuate somewhat on the world market, but all are close to the Euro.

This, then, has led to the increasing understanding of the obsolescence of national armies as institutions to keep the peace. More and more control in the past twenty years has been turned over to the United Nations and no major wars have been fought, although there have been some bloody conflicts involving United Nations Police in some of the smaller countries.

All Nuclear weapons are now in United Nations control. Here, too, General Amir played a major role. Negotiating tirelessly with his counterpart in India and each of them with their respective defense secretaries, a bi-lateral agreement was drawn up and ratified by both India and Pakistan, and all nuclear weapons and manufacturing facilities were turned over to UN control. One by one other nuclear nations followed suit until at last, just four years ago, the United States relinquished national control of its fearsome nuclear arsenal.

We did not reach the Peace of Jerusalem, but many are calling this phenomenal turning away from nationalistic warmongering and empire building "The Peace of Islamabad", recognizing General Amir's pivotal

The Message ◆ Part Two ◆ What, Then, Did Occur?

role in reaching this new era of world understanding.

THE WORLD SPIRITUAL COMMUNITY:

No single individual stands out in the coming together of the people of diverse faiths and religious persuasions. But one organization, Rotary International, has often been pointed to as instrumental in breaking down walls between the world's different religions. Many people, particularly Rotarians, have been surprised by this. This world-wide service organization, now with five million members, has always paid scant or no attention to religious differences in its membership or service programs. Perhaps it is just this which has made Rotary such a powerful force toward ecumenism.

More and more people are coming to recognize **COLLECTIVE CONSCIOUSNESS** as the ultimate reality, rather than looking at some more limited form of deity. Most use the term "God" rather than the rather cumbersome **"COLLECTIVE CONSCIOUSNESS"**. We are recognizing that each of us individually or in religious groups have only a limited view. And we see that **COLLECTIVE CONSCIOUSNESS**, though not omniscient, encompasses the totality of conscious entities throughout the universe.

ECOLOGICAL AND OTHER PROGRESS:

So much other change has come about in these past twenty years that I can here only point to the highlights. Turning away from reliance on national armed forces has freed up enormous resources for social and cultural and economic development. Though there will always be poor people, there is no longer the abject poverty which ravaged Africa and other parts of this planet twenty years ago. Basic education is now freely available to all, as is basic health care.

Our decreasing reliance on oil and the development of hydrogen powered vehicles have led to a time in which our air is nearly clear again. We are cleaning up our lakes and streams and rivers, and the ocean is becoming healthier. Earth's population has stabilized at about eight billion people. We have a United Nations Base on the moon, and have begun a program to terraform Mars.

Even though **THE EVENT** did not occur, we are beginning to refer to our planet as **THE NEW EARTH**. The new temple in Khajuraho was given to the people of Earth by a group of businessmen in India, the fastest developing country in the world in these past twenty years. Kiran Verma's new poem, the seventh in a series of "Five Poems Concerning Lightning", written in his ninety-eighth year, dedicates this majestic temple and celebrates the people of **THE NEW EARTH.**

WarrenHall Crain
18 December 2034
Khajuraho

II.

Aashchariya—Wonder

I named her *Aashchariya,* which is the Hindi word for Wonder, Surprise, Astonishment. But we soon began to call her by a diminutive *Aasha,* which means Hope. All of these English equivalents are appropriate for this amazing girl who was born so little time ago and who continues to astonish and surprise and astound us and to fill us with wonder and hope.

In the second day of her life, after a long night's sleep during which I lay awake with worry about this tiny girl who had come into my life, she told me her name. Yes, she began speaking only hours after her birth and by the second day was quite conversant, her English already better than mine and her Hindi nearly as good. Her name, which, after several tries we spelled "Pfththwgglr" seemed to me simply unpronounceable, though she spoke it glibly enough. She was pleased with my choice of a name which is easily pronounced in Hindi or English and it was she who suggested the diminutive for her *ghar ka nam* (house name).

I had gone to Mussoorie, I knew not why. I had simply had an overwhelming urge to be there, and

The Message ♦Part Two ♦ What, Then, Did Occur?

though my rationality could find no reason to go, I was learning more and more to trust my intuition, and I went.

When I got there my friends began to tell me about a strange event which apparently was about to happen. A thirteen-year-old street girl named Nitthu had been brought to the hospital apparently in the late stages of pregnancy. She adamantly professed that she has not had intercourse at all, that she was still a virgin. The doctors and nurses scoffed at this and almost angrily accused her of lying. Nitthu held to her story. Microsound showed that this was to be a multiple birth, with apparently eight fetuses, all very small.

The delivery was smooth and fairly normal and human. Though as I progress in this account you will wonder why I did not name this girl *Ajib* (strange). Soon we had eight infants, each apparently healthy, alive and well, wrapped in tea towels because these girls were too small for normal baby blankets. Each at birth about 15 cm. long and weighing about 1 kg. In those first few hours we worried a great deal about how these girls were ever to survive. They were so tiny and looked so fragile.

Somehow, I really did not know why at the time, I had been chosen as one of a small group of surrogate parents, or perhaps I might better call us guardians. And the girls somehow, even before they began to speak, divided themselves into three groups. *Aasha* came to me. Three others stayed together. And a group of four stayed together with another guardian.

All the girls were discharged from the hospital that

very day, there seeming to be no special care which they needed. Though, as I have mentioned, I worried mightily that first night until Aasha herself reassured me that all would be well, and on her second day took charge of her own life. As it turned out she did need a human guardian, but only to do the tasks which she in her tiny state simply could not do, such as going to the bazaar for supplies. By the end of the second day her birth weight had doubled and I expected her to be a fully grown woman in a few weeks. She laughed when I shared that expectation with her and she told me that, yes, she and her sisters (though using a different word as she said that their relationship was not really that of sisters) would be fully grown in about two months. Each would then be about one metre tall, and would look very like a young human girl.

I joshed with her and suggested that they must be from the planet Tralfamadore. That brought a hoot of laughter from Aasha. No, she said, quoting Kurt Vonnegut, there is no such place as Tralfamadore (Slaughterhouse Five, page 26). She and the others are indeed, extra-terrestrial, but not from another planet. Then she revealed to me the reason I had been chosen as her guardian and my feeling of amazement grew. Indeed I had named her well.

"Your friend WarrenHall Crain wrote a novel some years ago," she said to me, "which included a utopian vision of the future of Planet Earth." How she knew so many things I had begun to wonder. She seemed omniscient. And this was on only the second day of her

The Message ◆Part Two ◆ What, Then, Did Occur?

life here on Earth. "We eight girls are a creation of **COLLECTIVE CONSCIOUSNESS.** In its wisdom as the aggregate consciousness of all sentient beings in the universe **COLLECTIVE CONSCIOUSNESS,** as your friend realized in Part Two of his novel, had at the last minute aborted **THE EVENT** which was to have decimated Earth's population. Then, after a great deal of deliberation it was decided to give this marvelous planet guidance through these difficult years. We have come, we eight, as incarnations of **COLLECTIVE CONSCIOUSNESS.** Some, especially here in India, will realize that we can be seen as *avatars* of Lord Krishna. We are here not to take any power, but as preceptors and advisors, much as Lord Krishna was with Arjuna at the great battle at Kurukshetra. We are skilled in the arts of persuasion and will be able to gain audience with world and national leaders. Many of them will wonder why they are giving time to small girls. For so we will appear to people simply looking at us. Much as you wondered why you were present at our birth. We will not make any decisions or take any actions, but our advice will be strongly compelling. We believe and expect that it will be a major factor in the realization of your vision in **THE MESSAGE."**

There is little more to tell. The girls—we never gave them any more exalted title, simply calling them "the girls"—were born there at Landour Community Hospital in Mussoorie on Children's Day 2018 and lived on this earth nearly seventeen years. I was Aasha's guardian throughout those years, though I am now nearly a hundred years old. As you can imagine, Aasha herself guided me in the proper maintenance of a healthy life. She fully expects me to live to the auspicious age of one hundred and eight, in fulfillment of the Hindu ideal. The other guardians—two women, one with three girls and one with four—also stayed with the girls until that evening earlier this year.

Nitthu was honoured as their aunt, though she had given birth to them as a mother. They needed no maternal guidance. On the other hand, as you've already seen, the girls were guiding their guardians from the start. Few people, actually only the guardians and the medical people there at the hospital and, of course, Nitthu, know of this admittedly strange birth. Decisions were made very swiftly that there would be as little publicity as possible, to allow the girls to carry on their advisory work in the quietest behind-the-scenes manner.

Nitthu married soon after the birth of the girls. Her husband did not know that she was their mother, as they treated her as a respected Aunt. He knew little about the girls and wondered sometimes why they never seemed to grow up but always looked like little girls. The girls took charge of Nitthu's education and, though she was totally illiterate at the time of their birth, Nitthu became a very well educated woman and raised a boy and a girl who are now college graduates, the girl on the staff of All India Medical Services in Delhi, the boy a software engineer, graduate of Indian Institute of Technology Madras, and now employed by Microsoft at its main campus in the United States.

The Message ◆ Part Two ◆ What, Then, Did Occur?

Over the nearly twenty years that the girls were with us here they visited heads of state, business leaders, notable persons in the arts, literature, education, and religion. Few knew that these girls possessed the power of all the intelligence of the universe. Never did they make any demands. In fact, many a leader, after a visit from one of the girls, remarked that the girl had said very little. However, each found his/her thinking subtly changed, and the world bit by bit and visit by visit shifted to a new possibility of sustainable development, toward a world without war, a world without poverty, a world in which my vision is being realized.

I've spoken of my vision as if it is somehow mine. Aasha and I have laughed often about this as I soon realized the source of that vision. The vision which I call mine is nothing less than the vision of **COLLECTIVE CONSCIOUSNESS.** I was merely the vehicle bringing it into the world, as Nitthu was the vehicle bringing "the girls".

They were with us such a short time, these marvelous girls.

On the evening of the Dance Festival earlier this year we were all in Khajuraho. The eight girls and their three guardians. At dinner in the evening, before the dedication of the Temple of the People, the girls told us that they were leaving. They joked a bit with me in explaining that, though **THE EVENT** had not occurred, they were about to stage a **"MINI-EVENT"**. They went with us to the entrance of the festival. Indeed, we bought tickets. Children's tickets for them as we continued the subterfuge that these were little girls.

Then, just inside the gate, they simply disappeared.

My life was radically changed by the influence of this wonderful girl whose real name I never learned to pronounce properly. She was pleased with my choice of her human name *Aashchariya.* She was like a daughter to me and I was like her father, though the guidance which she gave me was far beyond any which I gave her. I had begun to call her *Aashch,* just a shortening of her full name, as *Aasha* (Hope) seemed too limited. She was so much more. Were I to name her now I would extend her name to *Aashchariya ka Upahar* (the Gift of Wonder).

Though very few knew that there was any outside interference in the affairs of humankind, **COLLECTIVE CONSCIOUSNESS,** in the persons of these girls, subtly and inexorably changed the course of human history. We now look forward to a future of peace and prosperity in which the vision of **COLLECTIVE CONSCIOUSNESS** is being fulfilled.

Kiran Verma
Independence Day 2033
Khajuraho

III.

The Temple of the People

Rs. 20 Crore (about forty million US Dollars) was the estimate we made in 2005 when I first broached the proposal for a new temple. I was sitting with the staff responsible for the maintenance of the Khajuraho temples. At first they simply said that it would not be possible. Then, when pressed, they conferred and gave me their estimate. None of them thought me serious. They did not then know me well and did not know that I am a man of dogged determination.

I mentioned this proposal that very afternoon to my dear friend Kiran Verma. He simply laughed and said, "*Han, hum karenge* (Yes, we'll do it.)"

Thus was the Temple of the People born. A vision alive only in the minds of two friends. Now, in gleaming new Panna sandstone, a floodlit reality, almost a twin to the one-thousand-year-old Chitragupta Temple next to which it stands. The Temple of the People has been built on time and on budget.

From the onset Kiran and I envisioned a temple honouring the highest and best aspirations of the people of Earth and especially the deepest religious traditions.

The Message ◆Part Two ◆ What, Then, Did Occur?

Little did we realize that the process of building was itself to be a magnificent testament to what we are now calling **THE NEW EARTH.**

WarrenHall Crain
September 2033
Khajuraho

IV.

Consensus

THE EVENT did not happen. That was the marvelous poetic science fiction fantasy of my dear American friend, WarrenHall Crain. *Aashchariya* and the other girls did not come. That was my own poetic science fiction fantasy. Both fantasies grew out of the limited vision into which Warren and I each sometimes fall and out of which most people live their lives—the belief that we are not going to make it without outside help. It so often seems, as it seems to most at the turn of this century, that any kind of positive, progressive future for the planet or for the individual is simply not possible without something from outside ourselves.

The events of these past twenty years show that this pessimism was simply misplaced. Human beings have within themselves, individually and collectively, all that they need. No outside help—neither the cataclysmic intervention of **THE EVENT** nor the almost surreptitious guidance of "the girls"—has been needed to bring us to this glorious period in the life of Planet Earth. We have named the new temple in Khajuraho *Janata Mandir* (The Temple of The People) because in this temple we celebrate the collective consciousness of Earth's people, the consensus which we feel on a global scale, the

The Message ◆ Part Two ◆ What, Then, Did Occur?

consensus which has been reached in innumerable smaller instances.

What is it that has made this global and local consensus possible? What has turned human society on this planet so radically around? How is it that we no longer treat each other as enemies and competitors but rather as fellow citizens on Planet Earth? How is it possible that we have reached "The Peace of Islamabad"? I see four factors, four reasons, four dynamics. And perhaps a fifth.

First, the "unthinkable" was becoming possible, indeed seemingly inevitable. At the turn of the century more countries were building or planning or hoping for nuclear arsenals. It seemed to many only a matter of time before a nuclear holocaust would occur on Planet Earth. World leaders and the population at large found this simply untenable. We decided, collectively and in many individual instances of consensus, to gain control of this monster so that we no longer needed to fear a nuclear conflagration which might have wiped out all life on the planet. This began with the work of General Amir in Pakistan and his counterpart, General Dwivedi, in India. When these two military leaders reached consensus and then when they included their nation's leaders in that consensus it was found possible to turn their not inconsiderable nuclear arsenals over to complete United Nations control.

Other nations, seeing this momentous breakthrough in Pakistan/India relations, began to move together, reaching agreements on issues between countries which had seemed intractable. Palestine and Israel quickly followed Pakistan and India. One by one other nations turned their nuclear armaments over to United Nations control. The United States, whom many feared would never relinquish these terrifying weapons, finally did just that. These steps led to the bringing down of the military establishments in every country as each country realized that they needed only a small police force. The security of the people of the world was no longer guaranteed by national force, but was in the hands of the United Nations Police.

When we found that it was possible to take these enormous steps we found ourselves taking many smaller ones as well. The freeing up of financial resources no longer needed to maintain individual national armed forces enabled us to tackle other problems which had seemed unsolvable. This led to a world of abundance in which we finally found a more equitable distribution of the world's resources and the elimination of severe poverty. This equitable distribution of the world's resources is the second factor in our progress.

A third major factor in bringing to fruition the vision of **COLLECTIVE CONSCIOUSNESS** had been the growth of the information society in which we live. This began with the development of the internet and the ease of communication around the world. As people learned more about other people in the world we began to listen to one another and to honour one another. We realized, in other words, that consensus serves us better than confrontation. And since we no longer had vast military means of confrontation we turned to consensus in our

The Message ◆Part Two ◆ What, Then, Did Occur?

dealings with one another.

The fourth factor was the end of the population explosion. With the leveling of Earth's population at around eight billion in the year 2021 we were able substantially to achieve the vision of **COLLECTIVE CONSCIOUSNESS** without the cataclysmic outside intervention of **THE EVENT.**

And there may be one more factor. Perhaps we were simply tired. Tired of fighting one another. And we decided, collectively, in the words of the old spiritual, "We ain't gonna study war no more".

We live now in peace and prosperity on Planet Earth.

Kiran Verma
18 December 2034
Khajuraho

EPILOGUE: ALWAYS

The rain falls gently again tonight
And there is no wind.
But in the skies above Khajuraho
Great sheets of lightning and jagged forks
Announce the beauty of your dance,
Lord Shiva.

Surely you are pleased with your people.
Yet again you are dancing in the night sky.
Tonight you revel with us in this, your temple
Honouring the people of **THE NEW EARTH**.

Rejoicing in a world where everyone has
Abundant food to eat;
Clean air to breathe;
Safe water to drink;
Where streams and rivers run pure and clear;
Where tigers roam the forests,
And great whales roam the seas;
A world in which health care is freely available to all;
Where everyone has a safe and secure home in which to live;
A world in which music and dance and the arts are flourishing;
And every person has access to superb education;
Where all people know you as the One God,
Though we still worship you in richly diverse forms.

Often you have come to us, in outward show, Lord Shiva,
In the clash and furor of the storm,
Phir bhi hamesha hamare dil main tu nachta hai. *
Yet always in our hearts you dance.

* I wrote this poem in Hindi. The last line is a translation of the next to last.

Kiran Verma
21 March 2033
at the dedication of
The Temple of The People
Annual Dance Festival
Khajuraho

AFTERWORD

A few hours after I had e-mailed the manuscript for
THE MESSAGE to my editor half-way round the world,
I texted her:

*I've been, in my head, composing AN AFTERWORD
for THE MESSAGE. My readers MUST know that
I am absolutely serious—that Kiran's vision can be—
MUST be—realised.*

Her answer:

Absolutely

Also by WarrenHall Crain

AASHISH 1926-2034
A novel. Torn from his family village near Lahore in the Partition of Pakistan and India, 1947, Aashish Kumar Chhaturvedi, a young Punjabi Hindu, flees as a refugee to India, where he strives to lead a life of passion and triumph until his death at age 108.
Copies of *Aashish 1926-2034* are available in print and Kindle formats at www.Amazon.com

READINGS FROM AN INDIA JOURNAL
101 entries from the author's personal India Journal. Of this book the author has written: When you read this book you will know, as the old Bollywood song goes, "Yeh mera India (This is my India). I love my India."
Copies of *Readings from an India Journal* are available in print and Kindle formats at www.Amazon.com

FUTURE CHRONICLES: THE FIRST 500 YEARS OF THE AGE OF SPACE
In process, to be published in 2017

TALES FROM EARTH ORBIT
Stories from 25 colonies in near-Earth orbit
in the Fourth Century of the Age of Space
In process, to be published in 2015

at www.poetsagainstwar.com
 Several peace poems

at www.emeraldcityrotary.org/crain
Our Man in India (despatches from India)
Our Man in Central Asia (despatches from Peace Corps service in Kyrgyzstan)

About the Author

WarrenHall Crain spent most of his boyhood years at Woodstock School in North India, as his parents were Christian missionaries in Burma. He holds a Bachelor of Arts degree from The College of Wooster and a Master of Divinity degree from The Colgate Rochester Crozier Divinity School. He has been a U.S. Naval officer, a Christian pastor, a consultant in time management and goal setting, and a telemarketer. Currently (2013–2016) he is a United States Peace Corps Volunteer in Kyrgyzstan.

For many years he has divided his time equally between India and the United States and considers both countries home.

See the WarrenHall Crain Author Central Profile at www.Amazon.com. (Link: http://amzn.to/1rmJ9Uq)

Website: www.WarrenHallCrain.com

CONTACT ME: wcrain@uw.edu

I'VE MADE STRONG statements in this book—particularly the five factors which have led COLLECTIVE CONSCIOUSNESS to the drastic action of bringing Earth's population down to two billion people.

This book is, of course, fiction. But I believe that it is urgent that we deal with these factors, as listed on page 9 of this book in THE MESSAGE to Joe and Molly—and that we deal with them soon.

Yet I am abundantly hopeful of a glorious future for human society. A future celebrated in Kiran Verma's great poem, shown in the Epilogue on page 105, and which is spelled out century by century in FUTURE CHRONICLES: THE FIRST FIVE HUNDRED YEARS OF THE AGE OF SPACE (Projected publication 10 September 2017).

Please let me know your thoughts.

Text me or **e-mail** me. My Kyrgyzstan phone number (until June 2016) is 1-996-770-550-721. And my e-mail address is wcrain@uw.edu.

Visit my **website**: www.WarrenHallCrain.com and **Join the Symposium** on Kiran Verm's vision.

Follow me on **Facebook** and **Twitter**:
www.facebook.com/WarrenHallCrain
www.twitter.com/WarrenHallCrain

I will reply to anyone who contacts me.

Warren Hall Crain
10 September, 2014

Made in the USA
Columbia, SC
26 September 2021